MR. KNOCKY

JACK ZIEGLER

MACMILLAN PUBLISHING COMPANY   NEW YORK

MAXWELL MACMILLAN CANADA   TORONTO

MAXWELL MACMILLAN INTERNATIONAL   NEW YORK   OXFORD   SINGAPORE   SYDNEY

For Beth M.,
a good friend of Mr. K.

First edition. Printed in the United States of America. The text of this book is set in 14 pt. ITC Garamond Light. The illustrations are rendered in pen and ink with watercolor.
10 9 8 7 6 5 4 3 2 1
Library of Congress Cataloging-in-Publication Data
Ziegler, Jack. Mr. Knocky / Jack Ziegler.   p.   cm. Summary: Having ignored the friendly, talkative old man who tells strange stories, a group of children is shocked when the man is hurt in an accident and begins to accept him and laugh with him instead. ISBN 0-02-793725-9 [1. Individuality—Fiction.] I. Title. II. Title: Mister Knocky.
PZ7.Z494Mr 1993   [E]—dc20   91-34145

The three o'clock bell had just rung and I was running all over the schoolyard, yelling at the top of my lungs.

Everybody knew what I meant. After all, Deep Dene is our favorite hangout, and when the call goes out we know what to do. We raced across the square, hid our books and lunch boxes in the whole school's favorite secret hiding place under the bandstand, and headed out to the edge of town.

Deep Dene. It's a magnet for us. In the summer we're there all the time, playing baseball, tag, catcher-flier's-up, Johnny-rides-a-pony—you name it. In winter we're there all the time too, sledding, ice-skating, building snow forts and defending them. Deep Dene has everything a kid could ask for.

But it also has a problem—old Mr. Knocky.

Don't get me wrong. Mr. Knocky is a nice guy. It's just that he drives us nuts.
He lives in a house on the heights overlooking Deep Dene and every time he
sees us coming down the path, he hops over his fence and runs right up to us.
"Hey!" he'll say, planting himself firmly in our path. "Did I ever tell you about
the adventure of the dinosaur and the opera singer?" And then he'll proceed to tell
us one of his long, complicated stories that never make any sense.

At first we tried to be polite and listen, but now we just cover our ears and run right past him.

He doesn't care. He just keeps yammering away and follows us.
Even during our games he runs from one player to the next, telling strange, crazy tales of moondogs, banana meatballs, talking sailboats, or the time he had lunch with a distant cousin of Mickey Mouse. He's impossible!

And when he's not busy talking, he's waltzing around or making funny faces at us or flapping his big arms like a duck. Did you ever try to have a good time when you're being hassled by a giant duck?

Of course, *he* always seems to be having the time of his life!

So on the day of the first snowfall we all went to Deep Dene. Larry, Mary Alice, Doug, Susie, Wendy, Billy Hanley, Whistling Pine, the Yakima Twins, Pianolegs Horowitz, me—you know, the usual gang. We got busy stockpiling snowballs, building fortresses and trying to ignore Mr. Knocky who, as usual, was babbling happily away about the high cost of airmail bologna or some such nonsense.

And when the first snowballs started flying, Mr. Knocky was right there in the middle of the battlefield, singing some stupid song about how hard it is to fit an airplane into a breadbox.

We did our best to avoid hitting him with any of our bombs, but it wasn't easy, what with him bobbing and skipping up and down our front lines. Finally, the inevitable happened. One of the Yakima twins hit him square in the noggin with a big bazoonga.

Down went Mr. Knocky, right in the middle of a rambling account of all the different kinds of doughnuts at the local Nosh-O-Mat.

When Yip Yakima saw what he had done, he was very upset. His brother Yap
tried to calm him down, but Yip jumped up and ran over to Mr. Knocky.

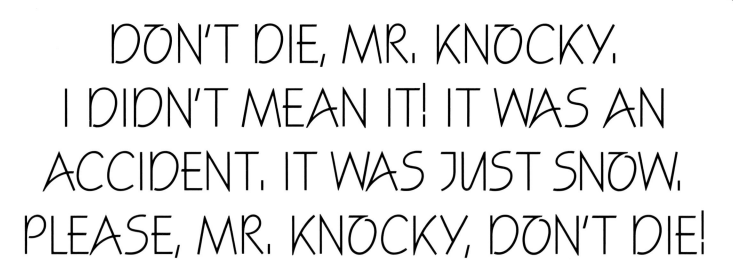

A stillness settled over Deep Dene as Yip knelt beside Mr. Knocky and started to cry. Yap climbed over the wall and stood next to his brother. Mr. Knocky lay as still as a stone. We all dropped our ammunition and gathered around the old man on the ground. You could have heard a pin drop if there hadn't been so much snow all around. No one knew what to do.

Well, we were so stunned to see that Mr. Knocky was still alive we forgot to cover our ears and get annoyed at all this goofy talk.

In fact, when he finally sat up and shook his head, we were so thrilled that we let out whoops of joy.

And then he started to tell us a couple of his long, stupid stories. One was a complicated tale about making mud pies out of apples and apple pies out of mud. The other was even weirder.

And you know what? For the first time ever, he had our full attention. As I listened I realized something: His stories *were* pretty dumb, all right, but they were also very, very funny. In fact, they were hilarious. And he had us all in stitches the rest of the afternoon.

We walked back to his house and he gave us hot cocoa and pretzels and some apple pie that tasted kind of funny, but was pretty good all the same.

Nowadays, whenever we go to Deep Dene to play ball or Johnny-rides-a-pony or have a snowball fight or whatever, we always call on our pal Mr. Knocky first and ask him to please, please, please come along. And you know what he always answers?

Well, what do you think?